Eric Carle
DREAM SNOW

Philomel Books   New York

On a small farm there lived a farmer.
He had only a few animals.
He could count them on the fingers of one hand.
So the farmer named his animals One, Two, Three, Four and Five.

By the end of the barn stood a small tree.
The farmer named it Tree.
"Hello, Tree," he would say when he passed it.

The farmer took good care of One, Two, Three, Four and Five.
Every day he fed them and cleaned their stalls.
In the evening, when his farm work was done …

… he went to his house.

Then he sat in his favorite chair,
drank a cup of hot peppermint tea
and ate a slice of bread with honey on it.
One night as he sat there …

the farmer felt very cozy and a bit tired.
"Heavens!" he said, yawning. "It's almost Christmas
and it hasn't snowed yet."
With that he fell asleep.

Soon he dreamed of falling snowflakes.
They gently covered him with a white blanket.

The snowflakes gently covered One with a white blanket.

The snowflakes gently covered Two with a white blanket.

The snowflakes gently covered Three with a white blanket.

The snowflakes gently covered Four with a white blanket.

The snowflakes gently covered Five with a white blanket.

The farmer woke up from his dream,
looked out of his window and saw snow.
It was not dream snow. It was real snow.
It had snowed while he had napped.

Now the snow clouds had moved away.
The moon and stars sparkled in the wintry night sky.

One, Two, Three, Four and Five were safe and fast asleep.

"Oh my! Oh my!" cried the farmer. "I almost forgot."
Quickly he put on his warm coat, his warm boots,
his warm hat and his warm gloves.

He grabbed a box, slung a sack over his shoulder and dashed outside.

Running past One, Two, Three, Four and Five, the farmer shouted,
"I almost forgot! I almost forgot!" waking up the animals.
They looked and wondered what the farmer was up to now.

They watched as he unpacked the box and emptied the sack.

One, Two, Three, Four, and Five watched as he decorated Tree.
Then he shouted, **Merry Christmas to all!**
And pushed the button.